Teggs is no ordinary dinosaur –
he's an **ASTROSAUR!** Captain of
the amazing spaceship DSS *Sauropod*,
he goes on dangerous missions and
fights evil – along with his faithful
crew, Gipsy, Arx and Iggy.

For more astro-fun visit the website

www.stevecolebooks.co.uk

Read all the adventures of
Teggs, Gipsy, Arx and Iggy!

Read all the adventures of Teggs, Blink
and Dutch at Astrosaurs Academy!

Find out more at www.stevecolebooks.co.uk

Astrosaurs

THE STAR PIRATES

Steve Cole

Illustrated by Woody Fox

RED FOX

THE STAR PIRATES
A RED FOX BOOK 978 1 849 41257 5

First published in Great Britain by Red Fox,
an imprint of Random House Children's Publishers UK
A Random House Group Company

First Red Fox edition published 2007
This edition published 2010

5 7 9 10 8 6 4

Text copyright © Steve Cole, 2007
Cover illustration and cards © Dynamo Design, 2007
Map visual © Charlie Fowkes, 2007
Illustrations by Woody Fox,
copyright © Random House Children's Books, 2007

Typeset in Bembo MT Schoolbook by Palimpsest Book Production Limited,
Polmont, Stirlingshire

Red Fox Books are published by Random House Children's Publishers UK
61–63 Uxbridge Road, London W5 5SA

www.**randomhousechildrens**.co.uk

www.randomhouse.co.uk

Addresses for companies within The Random House Group Limited can
be found at: www.randomhouse.co.uk/offices.htm

THE RANDOM HOUSE GROUP Limited Reg. No. 954009

A CIP   ish Library.

Per   ture for
our   ade from

For Shannon Park,
Teggs's auntie

WARNING!

THINK YOU KNOW ABOUT DINOSAURS?

THINK AGAIN!

The dinosaurs . . .

Big, stupid, lumbering reptiles. Right?

All they did was eat, sleep and roar a bit. Right?

Died out millions of years ago when a big meteor struck the Earth. Right?

Wrong!

The dinosaurs weren't stupid. They may have had small brains, but they used them well. They had big thoughts and big dreams.

By the time the meteor hit, the last dinosaurs had already left Earth for ever. Some breeds had discovered how to travel through space as early as the Triassic period, and were already enjoying a new life among the stars. No one has found evidence of dinosaur technology yet. But the first fossil bones were only unearthed in 1822, and new finds are being made all the time.

The proof is out there, buried in the ground.

And the dinosaurs live on, way out in space, even now. They've settled down in a place they call the Jurassic Quadrant and over the last sixty-five million years they've gone on evolving.

The dinosaurs we'll be meeting are

 part of a special group called the Dinosaur Space Service. Their job is to explore space, to go on exciting missions and to fight evil and protect the innocent!

These heroic herbivores are not just dinosaurs.

They are *astrosaurs*!

NOTE: The following story has been translated from secret Dinosaur Space Service records. Earthling dinosaur names are used throughout, although some changes have been made for easy reading. There's even a guide to help you pronounce the dinosaur names on the next page.

Talking Dinosaur!

How to say the prehistoric
names in this book . . .

STEGOSAURUS – *STEG-oh-SORE-us*

TRICERATOPS – *try-SERRA-tops*

HADROSAUR – *HAD-roh-sore*

IGUANODON – *ig-WA-noh-don*

ALLOSAURUS– *AL-uh-SORE-us*

DIMORPHODON – *die-MORF-oh-don*

SPINOSAURUS – *SPY-nuh-SORE-us*

AMMONITE – *AM-oh-NITE*

PTEROSAUR – *TEH-roh-sore*

MUSSAURUS – *moose-SORE-us*

CARNOTAUR – *kar-noh-TOR*

SAUROPELTA – *SORE-oh-PEL-tah*

KENTROSAURUS – *KEN-troh-SORE-us*

RAPTOR – *RAP-tor*

THE CREW OF THE DSS SAUROPOD

**CAPTAIN
TEGGS STEGOSAUR**

ARX ORANO,
FIRST OFFICER

GIPSY SAURINE,
COMMUNICATIONS
OFFICER

IGGY TOOTH,
CHIEF ENGINEER

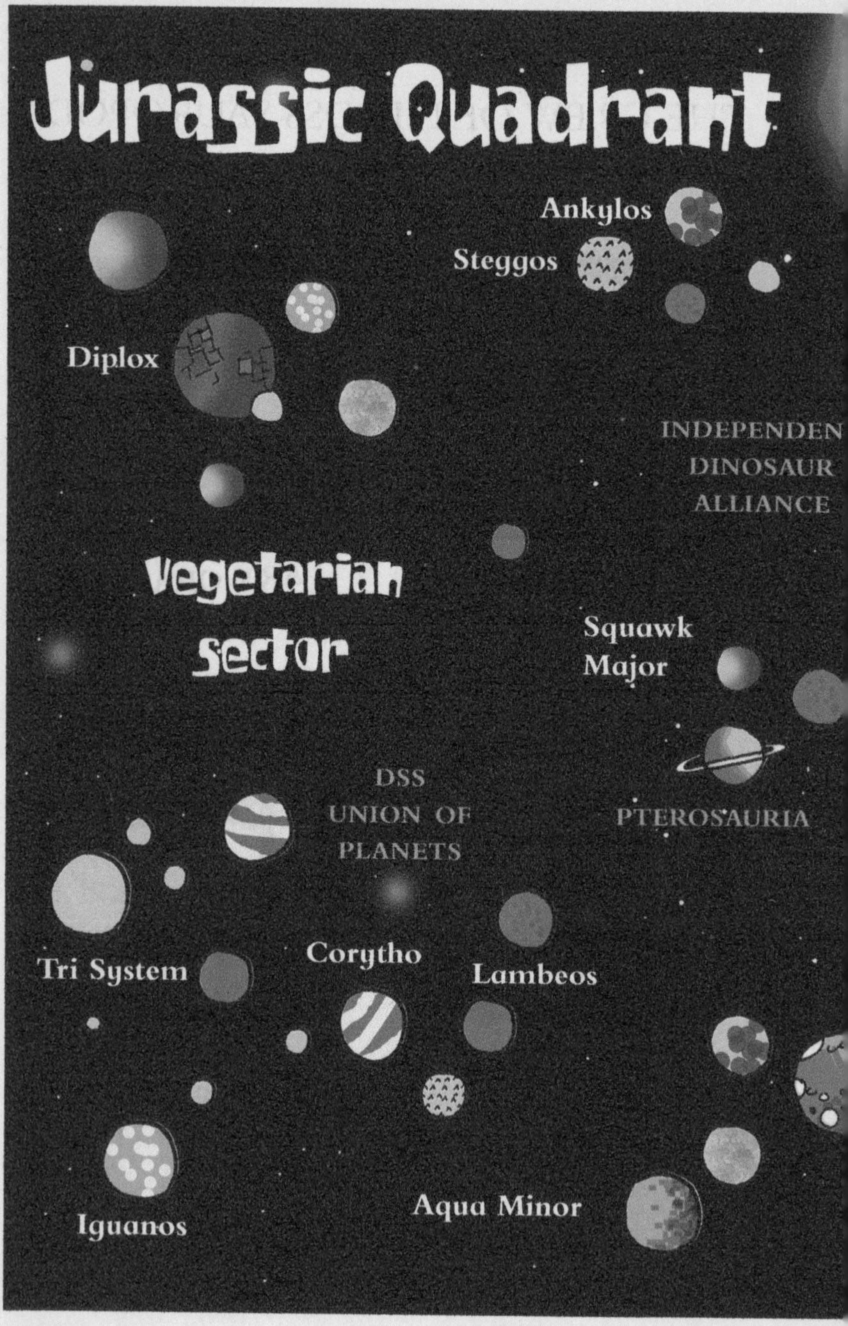

Jurassic Quadrant

Ankylos

Steggos

Diplox

INDEPENDEN
DINOSAUR
ALLIANCE

vegetarian
sector

Squawk
Major

DSS
UNION OF
PLANETS

PTEROSAURIA

Tri System

Corytho

Lambeos

Iguanos

Aqua Minor

Geldos Cluster

Teerex
Major

Olympus

TYRANNOSAUR
TERRITORIES

Planet Sixty

carnivore
sector

Raptos

THEROPOD EMPIRE

Megalos

Cryptos

vegmeat
zone

(neutral space)

SEA REPTILE
SPACE

Pliosaur
Nurseries

Not to scale

THE
STAR PIRATES

Chapter One

INVISIBLE ATTACK

Way out in the dark depths of space, a stegosaurus and a triceratops were waiting in a rusty old spaceship.

Waiting for someone to attack them!

"This ship is total rubbish," declared Captain Teggs Stegosaur. He tried to sit in a dusty chair but it broke beneath him and he landed on his bottom. "I never saw such a useless bag of bolts!"

3

"Me neither," agreed the triceratops, whose name was Arx. "The guns don't work, the steering is dodgy, and the engines so weedy we could hardly outrun a space-tortoise."

"True," Teggs agreed with a crooked grin. "It's perfect for our plan!"

"I just hope the plan works," said Arx grimly, checking his space armour. "If it doesn't, we are in big trouble!"

Teggs checked his own battle gear and looked out of the window at the comforting egg-shaped sight of the DSS *Sauropod*. The *Sauropod* was the finest ship in the Dinosaur Space Service. Teggs was its captain and Arx was his deputy. The rest of the

4

crew were still on board, awaiting their captain's signal.

He spoke into his communicator. "Teggs calling Gipsy. Are you there?"

"Gipsy here, Captain," came the reply. Gipsy was the stripy hadrosaur in charge of the *Sauropod*'s communications. "Iggy's here too."

Teggs smiled. Iggy the iguanodon was his Chief Engineer and very handy in a fight. "Hello, Iggy," said Teggs. "Any sign of enemy ships in the area?"

"Not yet, Captain," came Iggy's gruff voice. "But we've boosted the scanners and are checking them all the time. If so much as a miniature Martian moth flaps anywhere near you, we'll pick it up."

"I wouldn't if I were you," Teggs told him. "Those Martian moths can bite!" He started to chomp on a big pile of juicy leaves he'd brought over from the *Sauropod* canteen. The only thing bigger than Teggs's appetite was his sense of adventure! But even he had to admit that it was a funny feeling, sitting in a parked spaceship just waiting to be attacked by forces unknown . . .

"All right, everyone," said Teggs through a mushy green mouthful. "Let's run through the plan one more time. It's vital we all know what we are doing here."

Arx cleared his throat. "We are here because several spaceships have disappeared in this sector. They were all small ships with hardly any defences, carrying big cargos of electronic parts on board. The ships have never been seen again — but bits of their cargos *have* turned up on other planets."

"And that can only mean one thing," Gipsy added. "Those ships were hijacked, their crews were kidnapped – and anything valuable on board was sold off."

"It's a terrible business," said Teggs. "And *we* are going to put a stop to it."

"Yes, sir," said Iggy. "We know that those sneaky crooks would never dare take on a ship as big and strong as the *Sauropod*. But if they spy a rusty old cargo ship like the one you and Arx are on, chances are they will pick a fight. You're sitting ducks!"

Teggs looked at the broken chair and

sighed. "Or standing ducks, anyway,"
he said. "So – what's the plan, Gipsy?"

"While your crummy craft stays
parked in open space, we will hide the
Sauropod behind the nearest moon and
wait," said Gipsy. "If anyone *does* show
up and attack you, we will zoom out
of hiding and catch them red-clawed!"

"Very good," said Teggs approvingly.
He didn't only have the best ship in
space – he had the best crew too!

"Captain!" said Arx suddenly. He tapped a grimy computer screen with his biggest horn. "According to these readings, we are moving."

"But we are parked in space," Teggs argued. "How *can* we be moving?"

"I don't know," said Arx. "But we are!"

"Iggy," Teggs snapped into his communicator. "Is there anything showing on the *Sauropod* scanners that might be affecting us?"

"Can't see anything, Captain," Iggy reported. "No black holes or space tunnels in the area."

"Something is definitely pulling us away!" Arx insisted.

Teggs knew Arx was right. He could feel strange vibrations under his feet. He looked out of the window, but there was nothing out there but space.

He blinked, then gasped. Mysterious black smoke had started swirling around outside . . .

"Iggy!" Teggs shouted. "Gipsy, can you hear me? It looks like we've been pulled into a cloud of smoke!" But his only reply was crackly static. "Uh-oh. Arx, we've lost contact with the *Sauropod*!"

Arx joined him by the window. For a minute, the smoke cleared – and they saw a massive space station looming up ahead of them.

"No wonder Iggy and Gipsy couldn't see anything on the scanners," said Arx. "That stuff out there must be a smoke screen that doesn't show up on space radar. It hides our enemies from view while they drag spaceships into their lair!"

Teggs nodded grimly. That sinister lair was built from blood-red metal and shaped like an enormous hook. As he watched, a big, dark doorway opened up to draw in their little spaceship.

Etched in black above the doorway was a sinister symbol – a huge carnivore

skull with two broken bones crossed beneath it.

Arx gulped. "I recognize that symbol."

"So do I," said Teggs. "It's the sign . . . of the star pirates!"

A shiver passed through Teggs's long backbone. *Star pirates.* As a dino-tot he had heard so many stories about these scaly pirates of the stars – cruel carnivores that roamed space in search of ships to loot. Brave astrosaurs had hunted them down years ago, and so most were safely locked away. But some believed that the worst of the star pirates had escaped and gone into hiding – and that one day the devilish dinosaurs would return and take revenge on the whole Jurassic Quadrant . . .

"Well, we wanted to be attacked, and we were," said Teggs. "But our clever trap has backfired." A fearsome thumping and banging started up at the little spaceship's doors. "The star pirates have sucked the ship inside their space station, and now they're coming to get *us*!"

Chapter Two

PRISONERS OF THE PIRATES!

Suddenly the pounding at the doors
stopped. "Work together, me hearties!"
came a deep, growling voice. "We'll
charge that door on the count of three.
One . . ."

Teggs rushed over to the control
room's battered doors. "If the star
pirates want to get in, who are we stop
them?" he cried.

"*Two* . . ."

Teggs's tail hovered over the door
control. "Ready for action, Arx?"

Arx nodded bravely. "Ready,
Captain."

"*Three!*"

Bellowing a battle cry, the pirates charged forward – just as Teggs opened the door.

"Whoaaaa!" With nothing to block their way, the charging dinosaur pirates came tumbling into the control room, *out* of control. There were twenty of them at least, all different dinosaur breeds. And a right motley bunch they looked too – scabby and scarred, wearing tatty scraps of clothing.

As the pirates milled around in surprise, Teggs whacked the broken chair with his tail and sent it flying towards them. It landed on the foot of an allosaurus, who yelped in pain. At the same time, Arx lowered his armoured head and charged through the bemused bundle. He gasped – they smelled like they bathed in old dung every day and washed it off with slug juice!

"Good work, Arx," said Teggs as they pelted down a dark metal tunnel. "So much for the star pirates – what a rotten lot!"

But he was going so fast that he didn't see a rope net lying on the floor. As he ran over it – *WHOOSH!* – it scooped him up and dragged him into the air!

"Captain!" cried Arx. He stared helplessly at Teggs, dangling from the ceiling. But before he could do

16

anything to help, a large golden cutlass
was held against his horns.

"So – a rotten lot, are we?" It was the same low, growling voice they had heard before – but now it was right in Arx's ear. "Well, rotten or not, I reckons we have done for you two sonny jim-lads, and no mistake!"

Up in his net, Teggs frowned. "Er, pardon?"

"You are now helpless prisoners," boomed the voice. "Your fate is in my claws – the claws of Spiny Jim and his black-hearted pirate crew!"

Suddenly the lights switched on, and Teggs blinked. From up here he could see that he and Arx had blundered into a large metal wrecking yard, filled with broken-down spacecraft. *This* must be where all the disappearing ships had ended up – sucked in and smashed up by the star pirates!

And there below, pointing his deadly golden sword at Arx, was the strange, sinister figure of Spiny Jim.

The pirate captain was a spinosaurus. He had a face like a crocodile's, with sharp teeth that seemed to be made of solid gold. A spiky, spiny sail of skin stretched down the length of his dark grey back. He looked every bit the pirate with his wooden leg, gold hoop earring and eye patch. His right eye was uncovered and glinted in the light – it was made from glass!

A small pterosaur on his shoulder wore an eye patch too. "SQUAWK!" it cried. "You got 'em, Cap'n! You got 'em!"

"Shut your beak, Pollysaurus!" snarled Spiny Jim. "You make my ear ache!"

Suddenly, the other pirates came shuffling along with angry expressions on their faces. They were led by a mussaurus – usually a plant-eating dinosaur. But with a chill, Teggs saw that its teeth had been sharpened to white points, more suited to tearing meat apart than chewing leaves and grass. It had a hook instead of a hand and a red hanky wrapped around its head.

"You messed up, Mutty," scolded Spiny Jim. "But I got them for ye."

"That you did, Cap'n," agreed Mutty the mussaurus.

"How can you even see us, Spiny Jim?" Teggs shouted. "One eye is covered up and the other is made from glass!"

"I lost me own eyes in a fight," Spiny Jim admitted. "So I borrowed an eye from Pollysaurus here and stuffed it up my nostril!"

He lifted up his big grey snout and

21

Teggs saw a little red eye was indeed stuck there. "Eurgh!" said Teggs. "That's disgusting!"

"I said the same when he did it," Pollysaurus agreed. "Well, actually, I said, 'OWWWWWWW!'"

Spiny Jim gave him a swipe around the head. "Shut up, you mangy dino-bird, or I'll pull off your wings and stick them in my hat."

"But you're not wearing a hat," Arx pointed out.

"Phew!" said Pollysaurus.

"Look at our prisoners' armour, Cap'n," said Mutty. "They is astrosaurs, I'm thinking. Like them dreary DSS dino-dingbats who tried to put us all in prison."

"Wait!" Spiny Jim looked closely at Arx's belt buckle. "Be that . . . *gold*?"

"Er, yes," said Arx. "So?"

But the next moment, Spiny Jim swiped the buckle clean off Arx's belt with his cutlass.

"Hey!" Arx shouted. "I won that buckle at Astrosaurs Academy for being Brainiest in Class. It's special."

"Of course it's special!" cried Spiny Jim, holding it to his heart. "It's gold! Ha-harr! Oh, I loves gold." He started kissing the precious metal. "Gold, gold, glorious goldy-gold gold."

"Anyway, Mutty, you are right – we

are astrosaurs," Teggs shouted defiantly as the other pirates started to growl and hiss. "And prison is where you all belong!"

A big "Oooooh!" of outrage went up from the pirates. One of them poked Teggs in the bottom with his sword.

"Steady, lads," said Spiny Jim, sticking the gold in his pocket. "These astrosaurs are going to make our dreams come true."

"What do you mean?" Arx demanded.

"You is going to be held to ransom, me beauties," Spiny Jim went on, waggling his cutlass. "Mutty, send a message to DSS HQ . . . Tell 'em that we will swap them the fine captain and his green tri-serra-plops for two of their new-fangled A-wave magnetrons."

"Is that all?" said Teggs, a bit put out. "Surely we are worth more than two A-wave watchamacallits?"

"An A-wave magnetron is a new device that the DSS have been testing," Arx explained. "It pulls precious rocks and minerals closer to the surface of a planet, making them easier to mine."

"That it most certainly do," Spiny Jim declared. "And I needs two of them before I can put my master plan into action." Teggs and Arx swapped worried looks as the pirate captain threw back his big grey head and laughed. "Them magnetrons will make me and my pirate band the richest dinosaurs in the universe. And thanks to you two, I won't have to try and steal them — they'll be delivered straight to my door!"

Chapter Three

A FEARFUL FATE

Back on the *Sauropod*, Iggy and Gipsy were starting to panic. The dimorphodon, Teggs's flight crew of fifty flying reptiles, were already in a flap, buzzing about the flight deck like mad mosquitoes.

"I can't believe that cargo ship just vanished!" Iggy protested. "One minute it was here, the next it was swallowed up by a big fat nothing!"

"Poor Teggs and Arx," said Gipsy with a sigh. "I hope they are OK."

Sprite, the leader of the dimorphodon, took time out from his furious flapping to give a heartfelt cheep.

27

Then a loud beeping sound started up. The dimorphodon froze in mid-flight.

"A message is coming through," Gipsy cried, hitting a switch. "It might be them!"

But it wasn't. It was a message from Mutty the star pirate.

"Avast there, ye astro-scum," he began. "This is the star pirates calling. We has got Captain Teggs and First Officer Arx, and if you don't do as we say you shall never see them again!"

'What do you want, pirate-pants?" Iggy demanded.

"We wants two A-wave magnetrons, me hearties," said Mutty. "Leave them floating in space in Sector Twelve and fly away. We will be watching. If you do as you're told, we will send your friends back to you in a shuttle."

"No," said Gipsy. "Give us back

Captain Teggs and Arx first, *then* we'll
give you the magnetrons."

"No way," growled Mutty. "Leave
them in Sector Twelve, like I say. If you
don't – or if you try to trick us in any
way – you'll never see your friends
again!"

Mutty's laughter was so loud that Gipsy had to yank off her headphones. Then came a bleep that was even louder. "The pirates have stopped transmitting," she said.

"Send a reply, Gipsy," urged Iggy. "Tell them we'll give them what they want. We'll get on to DSS HQ straight away and get hold of those magnetrons."

She looked at him in surprise. "You mean you trust them to do as they say?"

"I don't trust them a millimetre!" Iggy replied.

He clenched his claws into fists. "But I've got a plan, Gipsy. We'll get back Captain Teggs and Arx, you'll see – and give these stupid star pirates a surprise they'll never forget!"

Back on the star pirates' space station, Teggs had been cut down from the rope net and was now being marched along a dark corridor. Arx was just behind him. Both of them had been stripped of their armour, poked by spikes and threatened with swords, and Teggs was getting very fed up.

Just then a loud beep came from Mutty's communicator. He chuckled nastily. "'Tis a message from the DSS, Cap'n," he rasped. "It says that they are dropping off the magnetrons right now. You will have them before this day is through!"

The crowd of pirates cheered at the news.

Spiny Jim turned to a large ammonite, which looked like a big swirly shell with something wet and nasty inside. It wore a little tank of water on its back and a diver's mask to stop too much air getting in. "Go to the control room, Alan," ordered Spiny Jim. "Set a course for Sector Twelve and get ready to suck in those magnetrons."

"Aye-aye, Cap'n," said Alan in a slimy, slithery voice. Then he rolled off down the corridor like a weird wheel.

Teggs gave Spiny Jim a stern look. "So – when are you going to let us go?"

Pollysaurus laughed, and Spiny Jim looked down his nose at Teggs – literally. "Let you go, me hearty?" The eyeball stuffed up his nostril narrowed. "Why should we?"

Teggs glared at the wicked pirate. "Because my friends are doing what you want! You have to keep your side of the deal."

"Not likely, me old matey!" said Spiny Jim. "When I has them magnetrons, no one in the universe will be able to stop my terrible plans a-coming true!"

"Let's eat 'em, Cap'n!" bellowed a pirate. Teggs and Arx looked at each other in alarm.

But Spiny Jim shook his head. "No, me hearties. I have a NASTIER fate in mind for these two space-swabs. They are going to . . . walk the plank!"

The star pirates laughed and cheered, and soon the shout went up: "*Walk the plank! Walk the plank!*"

"But the DSS might be tricking you," Arx cried. "What if those magnetrons don't work?"

"Right," Teggs agreed. "Wouldn't it

make more sense to keep us alive as hostages?"

"Sense?" said Spiny Jim, turning up his nose. "Yuk! Do what you want, when you want, and never wash yer hands afterwards – that's the star pirates' motto!"

The pirates cheered and shouted their agreement. All too soon, Teggs and Arx found themselves shoved into a large, smelly, circular arena. The walls were high with large ventilators set into them, close to the ceiling. In the centre of the room was a deep, dark pit with a long plank hanging over it, like a diving board above a swimming pool.

Teggs turned to Spiny Jim. "Is that what you did with the crews of those spaceships you stole?" he demanded. "Made them walk your stupid plank?"

"Indeed it was, me hearties," said Spiny Jim with relish. "For in the bottom of that pit lives the Venomous Splarg!"

Arx raised a bony eyebrow. "The who?"

"The Venomous Splarg!" roared Mutty. "It's our pet. Our ever-so-*hungry* pet!"

A fearsome sound – part-roar, part-belch, part hair-raising howl – rose up from the bottom of the pit, and Teggs and Arx gulped.

"Onto the plank with ye, Captain Teggs!" Spiny Jim cackled. "It's time to turn ye into pet food! *Ha-harrrr!*"

Teggs was pushed and shoved onto the wobbly wooden plank. He tried to turn back, but the pirates waved swords

and clubs and hooks in his face, forcing
him out further and further over the
smelly pit. Another terrifying roar
echoed out from under him.

"Off he goes, off he goes!" screeched
Pollysaurus, hopping up and down on
Spiny Jim's shoulder. "He'll soon be
pieces of *ate*! SQUAAAAAAWK!"

Chapter Four

ESCAPE TO DANGER

Helpless in the grip of two pirates, Arx watched in horror as his captain was poked and prodded towards the very end of the creaking plank. He couldn't let Teggs topple over the edge!

With a mighty roar, Arx swung his short, stiff tail like a club and whacked his captors on the back. They fell over with loud cries, and the other pirates turned round to see what was happening.

"Look at me!" Arx yelled, butting aside an allosaurus. "I'm escaping!" He ran off, skirting the edge of the pit as he raced for a set of doors on the other side of the circular room. "Catch me if you can!"

Spiny Jim snapped his gleaming jaws together. "Catch that three-horned fool, me hearties! NOW!"

A dozen star pirates rushed to obey – leaving Teggs alone and perched at the end of the plank. He thought fast. Arx had bravely bought him time, and he had to make good use of it. But where could he go? The Venomous Splarg lay

below him, Spiny Jim and Mutty were blocking his way back . . .

"Looks like the only way is *up*!" Teggs yelled. Taking a deep breath, he bounced up and down on the end of the plank, just like a diver on a diving board. Then, with all his strength, he took off into the air like a spiky orange missile!

"Catch the sticky-saurus too!" roared Spiny Jim.

Teggs went zooming upwards, spinning his long tail behind him like a propeller. He just managed to grab hold of a ledge in the curved metal wall. Below him, the pirates were shouting angrily and waving their claws. But that was good — because while they were doing that, Arx was able to make his getaway. The triceratops lowered his head and charged the double doors, knocking them right off their hinges.

"Keep running, Arx!" Teggs yelled. "I'll join you soon!"

"The only thing you'll be joining is bones in the Splarg's stomach, Teggs!" growled Spiny Jim. "Bring him down, Mutty."

Mutty pulled a laser gun from his pocket and opened fire!

Teggs gasped as deadly red laser beams started zapping into the wall all around him. The metal began to smoke and sizzle – and he knew that he would be next, unless he could reach one of the air vents above . . .

"It's time to climb," Teggs decided. Daringly, using the spikes on the end of his tail as hooks, he started to pull himself up the wall. The holes that Mutty was blasting into the metal were actually a big help, because they gave Teggs hand-and-footholds. Soon he had made it up the mangled metal wall all the way to the air vents. The

pirates roared with fury, and the room echoed with the stamp of scaly feet and wooden legs.

"Sorry to spoil your little plank party, 'me hearties'!" Teggs shouted. "But I'm off!"

"There's no escape for ye, Teggs!" warned Spiny Jim. "Pollysaurus – *fetch*!"

With a menacing squawk, the one-eyed pterosaur flapped off from Spiny Jim's shoulder. Teggs quickly tore the cover from the air vent and ducked inside. He found himself in a round, rusty tunnel, and was about to dash down it when he stopped.

"Why am I running from a pirate's pet pterosaur?" he wondered. "I'm fifty times bigger than he is!"

Pollysaurus flapped about outside the air vent, glaring at Teggs through his single eye.

Then, without warning, he lifted his bottom and fired a dung pellet!

"Ow!" cried Teggs as the missile whacked him on the leg and started to steam. At once the air filled with the smell of cabbage and rotten eggs, and Teggs choked. "Ugh! That dung is totally toxic!" He turned

to run and another
potent pellet
popped out of
the pterosaur's
bot and
splatted on his
back. This one
smelled even
worse.
"What a
stink!" Teggs
gasped.
"Much more
of this and
I'll pass out!"

Pollysaurus gave a sinister
squawk of satisfaction. "Plenty more
where that came from!" he promised.

Holding his breath, Teggs staggered
off down the tunnel with the
pellet-popping pirate-pet hot on his
heels.

★

45

Meanwhile, Arx was still running along the blood-red corridors of the star pirates' space station. Only a few of the pirates were following him: the allosaurus he had barged aside, and two carnotaurs – one with a wooden leg, and one with two wooden legs and a wooden tail. Luckily, neither was a very fast runner, and there wasn't room for the allosaurus to push past them.

As he galloped along, Arx looked around hopefully for a hiding place. At last, turning a corner, he found a large black door to his left. He bundled inside as fast as he could and closed the door behind him.

It was dark in the room, but Arx could hear the pirates approach – *scamper-scuttle-THUD, scamper-scuttle-THUD*. He crossed his horns for luck . . . and the pirates carried on past the doorway. Phew!

Arx flicked on the light switch and saw that he was in a large storage area. Several crates were clamped to the floor and there was a hatch in the wall directly opposite. LOADING BAY FOUR was written on it in big black letters.

LOADING BAY 4

"This must be where the star pirates take in small deliveries direct from outer space," Arx guessed.

He was about to nip back out into the corridor and see if he could get back to Teggs, when a loud clanking noise came from the black door. It had locked itself shut!

"Attention," said a calm computer voice. "Hatch opening. Sucking in magnetrons. Repeat, magnetrons coming aboard."

"Oh *no*!" Arx cried. "If that hatch opens, all the air will be sucked out into space – and me along with it!"

He tugged on the black door with all his might, but it wouldn't open. Behind him, the thick metal hatch was already grinding open. Sure enough, air began to be sucked out of the loading bay. It howled past Arx's ears, faster and faster. He held on tight to the door handle, but already his grip was starting to slip.

Arx gulped. If he couldn't cling on, he would be dragged out to his doom in the airless wastes of space! Through the hatch he could see the billowing black smoke that kept the star pirates' space station hidden from view. Then two big metal tubes came tumbling inside.

"The magnetrons," Arx gasped.

Powerful clamps came out of the floor and held the metal tubes firmly in place. Arx felt his head start to spin as the last of the air rushed out. "Sorry, Captain," he whispered. "I can't hold on any longer."

Arx let go of the handle and went flying backwards towards the open hatch . . .

Chapter Five

FALLING THROUGH SPACE!

Just as Arx was about to burst through the smoke and go spinning into space, two hands grabbed hold of his feet and held on tight.

Arx looked back in amazement –
and saw that Iggy and Gipsy were
leaning out of the magnetrons! They
were wearing spacesuits and trying not
to get sucked out themselves.

Then a little pterosaur – also in a
spacesuit – flapped desperately over to
the hatch and pressed a button. It was
Sprite, the dimorphodon leader! The
hatch closed again and air started to
rush back into the loading bay.

"Loading bay sealed," announced the
calm computer voice.

Arx collapsed to the floor. Iggy and
Gipsy scrambled out of their metal
tubes and crouched beside him. Sprite
perched on his head and cheeped.

"Are you OK, Arx?" Gipsy asked
worriedly, pulling off her space helmet.

Arx smiled weakly. "I am now that
you are all here."

Iggy grinned. "We decided to hide
inside the magnetrons and give these

star pirates more than they bargained for!"

Gipsy nodded. "With their space station hidden by that special smoke, we knew it was the only way to find you."

"Best of all," said Iggy, "Sprite has got a transmitter stuck to his spacesuit so the *Sauropod* will be able to track us!"

Sprite proudly tapped the top of his little space helmet with his wing. But then he gave a squawk of despair, and started chittering at Gipsy.

"Oh no," she wailed. "The transmitter has *gone*. It must have fallen off Sprite's suit when he flew over to the hatch – and now it's out in space!"

"So the *Sauropod* won't be able to find us after all." Iggy sighed. "Where's Captain Teggs?"

"I'm not sure," Arx admitted.

Suddenly the black door clanked loudly.

"Quick, someone's coming," hissed Gipsy, and all four astrosaurs dived for the cover of the nearby crates.

Mutty entered the bay with a couple of battered old loading droids – even the robots wore eye-patches on this space station! He inspected the magnetrons, then spoke into a communicator built into his hook. "Mutty here, Cap'n. The DSS have sent a pair of tip-top working magnetrons." He chuckled. "They'll be hopping mad when they don't get their astrosaurs back in return!"

'They'll soon have more to worry about than that," Spiny Jim's voice rattled from the communicator. "*Much more.*"

Mutty grinned. "Even so, Cap'n, I'll feel happier when them astrosaurs is captured again."

"My Pollysaurus will soon stink the sticky-saurus out of them air vents," Spiny Jim declared. "As for the tri-serra-plops, why – I'll pluck out his horns and grind them into my porridge before this day is done!"

The pirates burst into deep, nasty laughter.

"Connect the magnetrons, me hearty," Spiny Jim went on. "Soon we shall be ultra-super-mega-rich – and the Jurassic Quadrant will lie in ruins!"

With a final snigger, Mutty gave a signal to the droids and they carried the magnetrons out of the loading bay.

Once they had gone, Arx peeped over the top of his crate, holding his horns protectively. "All right," he said quietly, "here's what we do. Iggy, you and I will follow Mutty and learn what the pirates are up to with those magnetrons. Gipsy — I think I passed a ventilator grille in the corridor outside. You and Sprite must get into the air vents, find Captain Teggs and stop that pongy Pollysaurus!"

"Got it," said Gipsy, and Sprite nodded his head. "We'll use our communicators to keep in touch."

Quietly, the astrosaurs crept from the loading bay and set off on their separate missions.

High, high above in the space station's maze of ventilator shafts, unaware that his friends were on their way, Teggs was still busy dung-dodging. He kept trying to thwack Pollysaurus with his tail, but every time he turned to aim, the pterosaur bombarded him with bottom-bullets. The air in the tunnels smelled worse than a raptor's pants.

"Surrender, sticky-saurus," jeered the dino-parrot, flapping overhead, "and maybe then I'll stop."

"I'll never give up!" Teggs promised, crashing on through the metal pipeline.

Then suddenly he came to a wall of black fog.

"The space station's smoke-screen supply," he realized. "Spiny Jim must pump it out of these air vents to top up the shields whenever he needs to." He turned to face Pollysaurus with a grin of triumph. "And if this stuff hides your space base from prying eyes, it will hide me too!"

Dodging a last dung pellet, he dived into the thick smoke. He heard Pollysaurus screech with frustration – but the pterosaur didn't follow him.

"You haven't heard the last of this," it squawked, flying away. "Spiny Jim will get you, just you wait!"

Ha, thought Teggs. But his relief didn't last long. As soon as he tried to breathe in the smoke, he started choking and coughing. "Ugh!" he spluttered. "This stuff tastes terrible. It's probably poisonous!"

Teggs stumbled on through the black smoke. His eyes were burning and his throat felt like it was on fire. Surely one of these shafts would lead him out of the smoke and into fresh air again?

WHAM! Teggs walked into something metal. Waving his tail about to clear some of the smoke, he saw he had wandered into a large, rusty lift. "Must be an old service lift," he said, peering at the controls. "If I take a trip down a few floors, I'll get out of the smoke and stand a chance of reaching Arx!"

Teggs hit the fourth button down.
First the doors squealed shut. Then,
with a scraping, scrunching noise, the
lift began to move.

Slowly at first . . .
Then a little
more quickly . . .
And then
suddenly it
plunged
downwards!

"The lift is
out of
control!" Teggs
gasped as he
felt himself
falling faster and
faster. "If I hit
the ground floor
at this speed I'll
be turned into
stegosaurus jam!"

Chapter Six

THE VENOMOUS SPLARG!

The lift kept dropping. Teggs knew he would go *SPLAT* at any second.

Desperately, he smashed the roof open with his tail. Then he hauled himself out through the jagged hole. The dark lift shaft burned with bright white sparks as the lift scraped and skidded against the metal walls – and Teggs glimpsed a metal ladder running up one side.

"One last chance!" he muttered. As the ground came rushing up to meet him, Teggs leaped off the roof and grabbed for the ladder. The rusty rungs bent beneath his weight, but he clung

on for dear life –
just as the lift
hit the bottom
of the shaft and
exploded!
Ka-BOOOM!
The noise was
incredible.
Concrete
crumbled and
metal turned
to mush. A
purple fireball
shot up from
the wreckage,
and Teggs felt
the heat of it
on his back.
"That was a
bit close," he
exclaimed. "Still –
at least now I'm
out of trouble!"

But even as he spoke, the ladder broke away from the wall.

"Oops!" Teggs shouted as he fell with a sooty clatter into the bottom of the shaft. "Ow. *Now* how am I going to get out of here?"

But then he realized that the explosion had blown a hole in the bottom of the lift shaft. There was another room on the other side. It seemed to glow with murky green light.

Suddenly, a terrifying roaring, belching, growling noise came from somewhere in the green gloom. Now Teggs knew exactly where he was. He had ended up in the bottom of the pirates' pit after all – and that noise was the howl of the Venomous Splarg! Even now he could hear it, all big and squelchy, dragging itself towards him . . .

There was nowhere to hide and no way out. But Teggs wasn't going down without a fight.

"Come on then, Splarg!" he yelled through the hole in the wall, shaking his spiky tail in warning. "Let's see what you're made of!"

And the next second, Teggs had his horrible answer as the Venomous Splarg shuffled into view.

It was huge – at least three times bigger than Teggs – and seemed to be made of lumpy green slime with the odd red feather sticking out here and there. It had three heads, and each one boasted two warty noses and a huge oblong eye. Of course, one of the eyes had an equally huge eye-patch over the top. The monster had two mouths, one on each side of its billowing body.

Teggs gulped as the disgusting
creature reached out two giant, slimy
paws towards him . . .

"Hello, my dear," said the Splarg
cheerily in a very high voice. "Are you
all right? Sorry about the big roar
back then, but I was really furious – I
just chipped a fingernail!"

Suddenly Teggs realized the Venomous Splarg wasn't reaching out to hurt him — she was showing off her lovely long pink nails.

"A chipped nail?" came another voice. "Let us file it for you!"

"Yes!" cried someone else.

A gaggle of figures rushed out of the green murk. They were plant-eating dinosaurs dressed in rags — a sauropelta, a gryposaurus, a kentrosaurus . . . They started fussing about the Splarg, filing her broken nail, stroking her slimy skin and delicately rubbing her feathers.

"Where did you lot spring from?" Teggs asked, bewildered.

"We are the crews of the cargo ships that were sucked in by the star pirates," explained the sauropelta. "My name is Sid. Spiny Jim stole our stuff and made us walk the plank . . ."

"Luckily I was here to give them all a soft landing," the Splarg explained. "I'm not really venomous, and I don't eat anyone. I eat the glow-moss that grows down here in the pit. We all do!"

Teggs noticed the softly glowing moss. He was starving, and helped himself to a huge mouthful. "How did you end up here, Splarg?"

"Spiny Jim kidnapped me too," she said sadly. "He dragged me away from my own planet when I was little, thinking I was some stupid monster he could use to scare his enemies." She sighed and shook her three horrible heads. "I mean – do I *look* scary to you?"

"Er . . . course not!" said Teggs quickly. "But if you're actually a Very Nice Splarg, why do you pretend?"

"Because if Spiny Jim found out the truth, he would throw me into space." The Splarg smiled down at her caring crewmates. "Besides, it can get very lonely in a pit! The more dinosaurs he chucks down here, the more friends I get."

69

"It's not so bad down here," Sid told him. "Since we can never go back to our planets, we've made a new home with the Splarg. It's actually quite cosy."

The Splarg smiled and tickled Teggs under the chin. "I'm sure you will be very happy down here with us. You've arrived just in time for our sing-a-sea-shanty night!"

"I can't stay here singing sea-shanties," Teggs protested, gulping down another mouthful of moss. "I have to find out what Spiny Jim is planning."

"Oh, *I* can tell you what that nasty little star pirate is up to," said the Splarg. "If you will stroke my lovely long hair in exchange . . ." She smiled. "Do we have a deal?"

"I suppose so." Teggs frowned. "Hang on. You don't *have* hair."

"Yes, I do," she said, and pulled a long, sticky hair down from her sixth nostril. "Here it is!"

"Oh. Lovely," said Teggs, pulling a face. And while he tried his best to stroke it, the Splarg explained the details of Spiny Jim's terrible plan . . .

High above the Splarg's lair, while Arx and Iggy followed Mutty and the magnetrons through the crimson corridors of the space station, Gipsy and Sprite had crawled inside a ventilator shaft and were looking for Teggs.

Suddenly, Gipsy heard a rattling noise ahead. It echoed through the thick darkness. Behind her, Sprite gave a quiet cheep of concern.

"Captain?" Gipsy hooted softly. "Captain, are you there?"

"AYE!" thundered a terrifying voice as the side of the shaft was ripped away by massive claws. Gipsy gasped as the light of the corridor flooded in – and then she gasped again at the sight of a scaly spinosaurus wearing an eye-patch, with a nasty little pterosaur dancing about on his shoulder. A tough-looking crew of dirty dinosaurs lurked behind him.

"Captain is here all right, girlie," snarled the scary figure, showing off his sharp golden teeth. "Cap'n Spiny Jim, to be exact – leader of the star pirates. And now ye are in BIG trouble!"

Chapter Seven

THE GOLDEN PERIL

Gipsy thought fast. "Cool," she said
with a big smile. "Just the captain I
was looking for!" Even as she spoke,
she was nudging Sprite away with her
foot – the pirates hadn't seen him yet,
and the longer he stayed free, the
better.

Spiny Jim scowled. "Ye are dressed in
a spacesuit, missy," he observed. "Where
did ye come from?"

Gipsy was glad her spacesuit hid her
astrosaur uniform. "I'm, er . . . a
stowaway," she said. "I was hiding on
board one of the ships you stole." If she

could only trick the pirates into trusting her, it would be easier to help her friends. "And now I want to join your band."

"Join us?" squawked the one-eyed pterosaur, flapping his wings.

"That's what she said, Pollysaurus!" Spiny Jim chuckled, and his crew roared with laughter. "Sorry, missy. We don't have girls in our gang, because girls be rubbish fighters!"

Gipsy whacked him in the chest with a hoof jab. As Spiny Jim staggered back, she whipped away his golden cutlass and cut through the belt in his trousers. They fell down around his ankles and tripped him up. The other pirates gasped in shock.

At once, Pollysaurus blasted Gipsy with a dung-ball. But Gipsy deflected the steaming missile with the golden sword and it landed with a splat in an allosaur's eye!

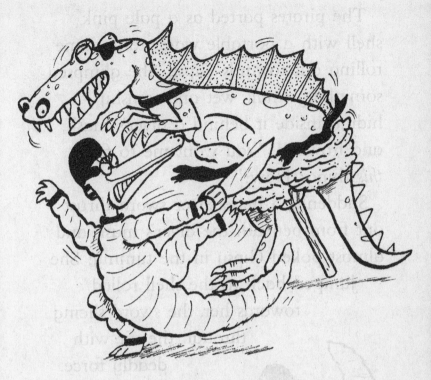

Amazed, the other star pirates wondered what to do. But then Spiny Jim got up and adjusted his trousers. "Well, girlie, perhaps ye can fight a bit," he admitted. "But if ye wants to join our band, ye must first fight the most fearsome swordmaster on board. The deadly, the diabolical . . . *Alan the ammonite!*"

The pirates parted as a pale pink shell with a portable water tank came rolling out towards Gipsy. She glimpsed something small, wet and squishy hiding inside it behind a diver's mask, and frowned. "You want me to fight *this* thing? How?"

Suddenly, a huge silver sword thrust out from beneath the diver's mask and almost poked Gipsy in the tummy! She jumped back as the shell rolled towards her, the sword slicing through the air with deadly force.

The pirates laughed and cheered.

"Many a dinosaur has underestimated Alan the ammonite," sneered Spiny Jim, slapping his wooden leg. "And many a dinosaur has wound up with one of these because of it!"

Gipsy gulped and gripped her golden cutlass as the killer shell came rolling towards her.

Alan swiped at her ankle, but Gipsy blocked the blow and kicked him away. The shell flipped up in the air and squirted salty water in her face. Gipsy wiped her eyes – in time to see Alan attacking again! She just managed to deflect his strikes, but he kept bouncing in the air, swinging his sword, driving her back towards the wall of the corridor . . .

Suddenly, with a super-swift movement, Alan whacked the cutlass from Gipsy's grip! Desperately she spun round in a circle and socked him with her tail. The blow knocked him across the floor – but all too soon he skidded to a halt. With a hiss he started rolling back towards her, sword extended, travelling at thirty miles per hour . . .

A second before he spun straight into her, Gipsy leaped high in the air. The ammonite went whizzing onwards – he couldn't stop in time! With a squeal, he slammed into the wall and the point of his sword got stuck there. Gipsy trotted over and brought her hoof down on the top of his shell. Alan fell to the ground with a crunch.

Gipsy picked up
his sword as well
as her own. "I'm
the winner!" she
shouted.

The other pirates
stared, speechless.
Then they cheered
and roared in
admiration, gave
her big hugs and
raised her up onto
their shoulders.
Gipsy forced a
smile. It looked like she had fought
her way into the star pirates' ranks.
But Teggs still needed help, and she
had no idea where Arx and Iggy
might be. What was she going to
do now?

In fact, Arx and Iggy were still
following Mutty and his two droids.

79

The pirate seemed to be taking the magnetrons into the very centre of the space station.

At last, he stopped outside a large golden door. Arx and Iggy watched as he tapped out a special security code on a keypad beside it. The door slid slowly upwards, and Mutty scuttled inside. The loading droids clanked after him with the magnetrons.

Keeping low to the ground, Arx and Iggy shuffled inside using the droids as cover.

"Wow," breathed Iggy, staring around. They were in a massive, gleaming control room – the walls, floor and ceiling were all made of solid gold. "This room must be worth a fortune!"

But Arx was more interested in what was *inside* the room. Big computers and banks of controls were connected by huge clumps of coloured wire. Another pirate, an old raptor, was running about between them, flicking switches and pushing buttons. Mutty went over to join him, peering at screens and studying read-outs.

"I recognize this equipment," Arx murmured. "It was taken from the ships the star pirates attacked. They've built this control room out of stolen electronic parts! But why?"

"And why use so much gold?" Iggy wondered.

"Spiny Jim is mad about the stuff," Arx explained.

The droids dragged the magnetrons towards a large slot in the middle of the floor. Arx and Iggy watched as they put them in place.

The control-room raptor chuckled. "Once the magnetrons are connected, the Gold Magnet will be ready at last!"

"Gold Magnet?" Iggy echoed.

"Oh dear," said Arx. "I have a bad feeling about this."

'We shall rip out the gold from every planet we pass," cried Mutty, hopping about from foot to foot.

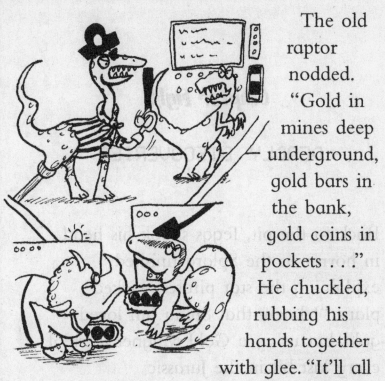

The old raptor nodded. "Gold in mines deep underground, gold bars in the bank, gold coins in pockets . . ." He chuckled, rubbing his hands together with glee. "It'll all be sucked up into space and stuck straight in our central storeroom. Soon we will be the richest dinosaurs of all time!"

Chapter Eight

DEADLY DISCOVERIES

Back in the pit, Teggs shook his head in horror as the Splarg finished explaining the star pirates' wicked plans. "I knew that Spiny Jim loved gold, but using a Gold Magnet to steal every last bit in the Jurassic Quadrant?" Teggs pushed the sticky hair back up the Splarg's nostril. "He's crazy!"

"He may be crazy but he'll never be caught," said the Splarg. "Thanks to the smoke screen around this space station, the star pirates can come up close to the planets they want to plunder and no one will ever know!"

"They'll leave every world in space poor and penniless," Teggs agreed. "We *must* stop them."

"How can we?" protested the Splarg. "There's no way out of this pit, believe me. I've been here for years and years, and I would know if there was—"

Suddenly, a big door opened up in the mossy wall behind her!

"Oh." The Splarg frowned. "How embarrassing."

Sid and the other cargo-ship crewmembers scurried away from the door, but Teggs held his ground. "Who's there?" he demanded.

And Sprite the dimorphodon flapped out!

"Sprite!" Teggs beamed and clutched the little pterosaur to his chest. "It's so good to see you. Where did you come from?"

"*Cheep*," said Sprite.

"You found a service tunnel leading all the way from the air vents to here?" Teggs cried. "Fantastic! Have you brought help?"

"*Chirp*," said Sprite.

"What? Gipsy and Iggy are here too, but Gipsy's been caught and is in the most terrible danger? Why didn't you tell me sooner? We must save her!" Teggs turned to the cargo-ship crewmembers. "Come on, everyone. You've been prisoners of the star pirates for far too long. Help me save my friend and defeat the star pirates – before they ransack the whole Jurassic Quadrant!"

Sid nodded. "We'll always be grateful to the Splarg," he declared, "but it's time we got our own back. We'll teach Spiny Jim to steal our ships, won't we, boys?" The other crewmembers roared in agreement, and rallied around Teggs.

The Splarg looked hurt. "But . . . you can't leave now!" Big teardrops welled up in her two good eyes. "It's sing-a-sea-shanty night tonight. I was going to make moss pancakes!"

"Come with us, Splarg," Teggs urged her. "If we beat Spiny Jim and his gang, you can go back home!"

"This pit is the only real home I know." The Splarg sniffed quietly. "Very well – push off and leave me alone!" She turned her back on them all. "I'll have a lovely time singing sea-shanties all by myself. Just see if I don't!"

The crewmembers looked sad, and Teggs felt awful. But there was too much at stake to spare the feelings of a lonely Splarg.

"Right then, boys," Teggs cried, charging through the wide-open door and into the cramped service tunnel. "It's time to spring a surprise on Spiny Jim and his potty pirates. There's not a moment to lose!"

Back in the Gold Magnet room, Arx and Iggy were still hiding behind the loading droids while Mutty and the raptor fiddled with the controls.

"We have to stop them," Iggy murmured, glancing at a screen behind them. "We are still in Sector Twelve. The *Sauropod* might be close by. If we could only make contact somehow!"

"I wonder," said Arx quietly. "I think I understand the Gold Magnet's controls. And if the *Sauropod* really *is* nearby, perhaps we could use it—"

"Use it how?" asked Iggy.

But before Arx could reply, the loading droids suddenly clanked away from the magnetrons – leaving the astrosaurs in plain view!

Mutty saw them at once. "Intruders!" he rasped.

The raptor jumped in the air, rubbing his claws. "*Dinner*, you mean!"

"I'll hold off them off, Arx," cried Iggy. "You fix the controls!"

The raptor bounded towards him. Iggy sent a burst of energy from his stun claws that knocked the raptor flying. But at the same time, Mutty pounced and brought Iggy crashing down to the floor.

Meanwhile, Arx charged over to the Gold Magnet's controls. He jabbed buttons frantically while using his tail to change the sensor settings on the magnetrons. He had a plan . . . but did he have enough time to put it into action?

Iggy struggled with Mutty, trying to get the pirate's hook away from his face. "You should be careful with that thing," he gasped, shoving the pirate back. "You might tear my uniform!"

"We'll do a lot more than just tear your uniform, me hearty," growled a voice behind him.

Iggy had a sinking feeling. He turned to find that a huge spinosaurus with a pterosaur on its shoulder was looking down its nose at him.

"Oh no," cried Arx, still fiddling furiously with the controls. "It's Spiny Jim!"

"Pollysaurus," snapped Spiny Jim.

"Stop that tri-serra-plops!"

Iggy gasped as the pterosaur flapped into the air and bombarded Arx with steaming dung-nuggets.

"Munch on these, horn-head!" screeched Pollysaurus. "SQUAWK!"

Arx was quickly driven back from the Gold Magnet controls, choking and gasping for breath – just as star pirates poured into the room. Mutty, the raptor, an allosaurus – even a crazy spinning shell – all grabbed hold of Iggy and forced him to his knees. Arx tried to help him but was sidetracked by a pair of carnotaurs.

"Arx, did you fix their machine?" Iggy asked hopefully.

"I was too slow," wailed Arx. "I didn't manage to do anything!"

"Well, well." Spiny Jim stared at Arx and Iggy as the pterosaur landed back on his shoulder. "Lucky we came along when we did. We was just showing our new pirate-girl the finished Gold Magnet," He looked behind him and whistled. "Come on, girlie, don't be shy!"

Iggy stared in amazement as a familiar figure charged up to him, waving a sword. It was Gipsy! "Leave this scaly space-dog to me, me hearties," she snarled, shooing Mutty and the other guards away.

Iggy gulped in alarm. "Are you feeling all right?"

"Better than YOU are going to be!" she snarled. "I'll teach you a lesson you will never forget . . ." She lowered her voice and winked at Arx. "A lesson in breaking out," she hissed. "I'm only pretending to be on their side. Get ready to make a surprise attack!"

"No, Gipsy," Arx told her loudly. "There are too many of them!"

"The green one knows her name!" squawked Pollysaurus. "She's an astrosaur! She's an astrosaur!"

"I— I'm not!" Gipsy protested. But Spiny Jim tore a hole in her spacesuit to reveal her astrosaur uniform beneath. "Thought you could trick me, eh?" he snarled, snatching Gipsy's sword away. "Well no one makes a fool of Spiny Jim."

"No one needs to," Gipsy retorted. "You do a fine job all by yourself!"

Spiny Jim shoved her towards Arx and Iggy. "You will pay for this," he rasped. "All of you!"

"Arx," groaned Iggy. "You gave Gipsy away! Why?"

But Arx couldn't – or wouldn't – answer. He could only watch helplessly as the star pirates closed in on the astrosaurs, their huge jaws drooling . . .

Chapter Nine

"ATTACK ALL PLANT-EATERS!"

"Wait!" Arx snapped. "Before you deal with us, at least give us a demonstration of your Gold Magnet."

Spiny Jim held up his claw and his pirates paused. "Why should I?"

"Because I think you've made the whole thing up," said Arx. "Gold Magnet? Pile of pirate pants more like!"

"We don't be making it up," hissed Mutty.

Arx waggled his horns rudely. "Prove it then!"

Iggy stared at Arx. What had got into the triceratops? First he had blown

97

Gipsy's cover. Now he actually wanted the star pirates to ransack a whole planet, just so he could stay safe a little longer!

"The magnetrons are plugged in, Cap'n," said Mutty. "The Gold Magnet is ready."

Spiny Jim nodded. "Then let's show these astrosaurs how we'll plunder the planets they've pledged to protect!" The other pirates roared in agreement and he laughed. "Right ye are, me hearties! Let's get a-guzzling gold!" He hobbled over to a big bank of controls and turned on a scanner. It showed a blue stripy planet. "The nearest world is Corytho. Lots of gold down there . . ."

"Look!" cried Gipsy, pointing to a familiar egg-shaped object close to the planet on the screen.

"It's the *Sauropod*," Iggy cheered. "I *knew* the crew would still be searching for us. But with the smoke screen up they will never find this stupid space base."

"This is perfect," snarled Spiny Jim. "We will steal all the gold on Corytho – right from under the noses of the DSS!" He pulled a big golden lever. "Here we go!"

A huge hum of power started up. The magnetrons glowed bright blue – even bluer than Gipsy's head-crest. "You can't do this!" she shouted.

"Magnetrons at full power, Cap'n," said Mutty, ignoring her.

The raptor ran about checking the controls. "Sucker systems set to maximum."

"At last!" exclaimed Spiny Jim. "We is going to get the rewards we so richly deserve!"

"NOT SO FAST!" came a ferocious roar from the golden doorway.

"Captain Teggs!" Iggy wiped his brow. "Just in the nick of time!"

The brave stegosaurus was holding a sword made from a bit of metal, and Sprite was perched on his head.

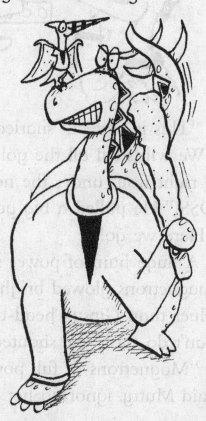

"Turn off that Gold Magnet, *Spineless* Jim," said Teggs. "And tell your crew to surrender."

"Who's going to make us?" growled Spiny Jim.

"We will!" yelled Sid the sauropelta, charging into the room. Twenty more skinny dinosaurs in rags followed behind him with more home-made weapons. The pirates gasped.

"But . . . you lot was all eaten by the Splarg!" Spiny Jim protested. "I saw you fall into the pit!"

"Plant-eaters are tougher than you think," said Teggs with a smile. "Nothing can stop us, least of all a pathetic pirate like you!" He pointed to the lever. "You are outnumbered, Jim lad. Turn off that machine right now!"

"No!" yelled Arx, shrugging off his captors. "Don't listen to him, Spiny Jim. Keep the magnet running. You can beat this sticky-saurus and his army of weeds."

"Arx!" cried Teggs in disbelief. "Have you gone space crazy?"

"The tri-serra-plops is right," Spiny Jim declared, raising his golden cutlass as the hum of the Gold Magnet got louder and hungrier. "Come on, lads, we can't stop now! *Attack all plant-eaters!*"

A fearsome fight broke out in the golden room.

The old raptor hurled himself at Teggs, who had to fight him off with the makeshift sword. Then two more pirates attacked him, and he had to use his spiky tail to keep them at bay.

Meanwhile, Mutty hurled himself at Gipsy. She jabbed him in the snout and kicked him so hard he flew across the room.

Iggy was attacked by Alan the ammonite. He blocked the blow with his stun claws, picked up the ammonite and hurled him like a discus. *CLONK!* The shell struck a carnotaur's head and knocked him into two more pirates.

While the dinosaurs battled on the ground, Sprite tangled with Pollysaurus in the air. The two pterosaurs bashed beaks and clashed claws as they spiralled around, struggling to gain the upper wing.

"Hey, Iggy!" shouted Gipsy, nose-jabbing Mutty in the back of the neck and making him yell. "Where's Arx?"

Then they saw him – shoving Sid the sauropelta away from the Gold Magnet's controls.

"I don't believe it," said Iggy, ducking the claws of an enraged allosaurus. "Arx has switched sides!"

Teggs scowled. "Arx, stop that. I *order* you to stop!"

"Sorry, Captain," called Arx. "I can't hear you!"

The golden room echoed with shouts, grunts and the clash of cold steel as the skinny crewmembers joined in the fighting.

"Give it up, Spiny Jim!" Teggs shouted, pushing his way through the battling scrum to get to the pirate captain. "We've got your gang on the run. You can't beat all of us."

"Your mate Arx doesn't seem to think so," said Spiny Jim. He bared his golden teeth and swiped at Teggs with his cutlass. "And now I reckon it's time you was cut down to size!"

Teggs blocked the blow with his sword – and then the golden chamber rocked, like something very powerful had crashed into it. Teggs staggered back and squashed Alan the ammonite with his bottom. Sprite and Pollysaurus bumped into one of the golden walls and tumbled to the ground.

Spiny Jim reared up in alarm. "What's happening?"

"You're getting the treasure you so richly deserve." Arx beamed as the whole space station rattled again.

"Remember when I said I didn't manage to do anything to your controls? Well, I'm afraid I was fibbing!"

"But the magnetrons are working perfectly," Mutty protested. "The whole system is working like a charm!"

"True," Arx agreed. "But you see, I changed the setting on the Gold Magnet's sensors. Instead of seeking out and sucking in gold, it is seeking out and sucking in . . . DUNG!"

Gipsy stared at him. "Then the Gold Magnet is now a *Dung* Magnet?"

Iggy gasped. "Anyone going to the toilet on Corytho is going to get a big surprise!"

Suddenly the space base rocked again and the lights flickered. "Is the dung doing that?" shouted Gipsy.

"Not just dung," said Teggs. Now, on the scanner, he could see tiny white missiles streaking away from the *Sauropod* towards them. "Look! Spiny Jim's Magnet is drawing out the dung *torpedoes* from our ship!"

"That explains the explosions," Gipsy realized. "They must be going off the moment they hit the storeroom here!"

Arx nodded as the room rocked and

the rich smell of dino-dung spread through the air. "It was the only way I could think of destroying the Gold Magnet for good. That's why I couldn't let anyone stop it being switched on. I knew the *Sauropod* would never find us because of the smoke screen — this was the only way that the dung torpedoes would definitely find their mark."

"Nice one, Arx," said Iggy as an ear-splitting *BOOM* went off beneath them. "The star pirates' space station is attacking itself!"

Gipsy gulped. "But we're still trapped on board!"

"I'll get you for this!" bellowed Spiny Jim. He jumped up, pulled out his sword and charged towards Arx . . .

But then the room lurched sideways.

Everyone was sent flying and black smoke started hissing into the glinting gold chamber.

"The smoke screen!" Teggs yelled. "The pirates store a fresh supply in the air vents so they can pump it out when they need to."

Gipsy nodded and started to cough. "The explosions must have damaged the controls. The smoke screen is being sucked inside *here*!"

Iggy stared around in alarm. "Soon we won't be able to see a thing!"

"Ha-harrrr!" said Spiny Jim. "But

me and my pirates know this space
station like the backs of our claws.
We can hold our breath, find our
way to the spaceship bay and escape
– while the rest of you stay here
and choke!"

"This way!" squawked Pollysaurus,
flapping above them. "This way!"

While the crewmembers milled
about helplessly, Spiny Jim rushed
after his pterosaur, his rascally band
of pirates hot on his heels. "Come
on, me beauties! HA-HARRRR!"

"It's not fair!" gasped Gipsy, her eyes

streaming. "Spiny Jim's right. He and his star pirates will get clean away while we are left behind!"

"The *Sauropod* might be able to find us now," said Iggy hopefully.

Teggs shook his head. "Even if they do, it will be too late." Another massive explosion almost split the room apart. "Even if we don't choke to death, we will soon be blown up – by our own torpedoes!"

Chapter Ten

HARD TO SWALLOW!

"Sorry, everyone," wheezed Arx. "Looks like my plan has gone a bit wrong."

"It was a good try, Arx," said Teggs. "Let's see if we can block the vents to stop any more smoke getting in."

"But where *are* the vents?" said Gipsy helplessly.

The black smoke was getting thicker. Teggs stumbled about in search of a vent, but only bumped into other dinosaurs.

There was a loud crash from somewhere close by — followed by a feeble "*Cheep!*"

"Hey, that sounded like Sprite!" said Teggs.

"It's all right, I've found him." Iggy gasped. "And that's not all – I think the poor little fella flew into the ventilator grille! There are some controls beside it . . ."

Teggs swept his tail around in a tight circle, using it as a fan to clear some of the smoke away. "Can you stop the smoke coming in?"

Iggy pushed the buttons. "They aren't

working! I'll try to fix them."

"I'll help you," offered Arx.

"Gipsy!" Teggs shouted. "Help me clear the smoke around the controls so they can see what they're doing!"

Gipsy hooted as loud as she could, blowing loads of smoke away. Sprite flapped his wings weakly, trying to keep the controls clear, and Teggs kept twirling his tail. His eyes were watering and he could hardly breathe, but he kept on going while Arx and Iggy worked as quickly as they could.

"Done it!" gasped Arx as a rushing, swooshing noise started up. At once the smoke was snorted back inside the vent.

"I've set the controls to reverse," explained Iggy. "The vents should spit all that smoke out into space."

A ragged cheer went up from the conked-out crewmembers, who were sprawled on the floor. But then the room rattled once again as yet another dung-flavoured explosion went off. "How many blasts have there been?" Teggs wondered.

Gipsy coughed and wiped her eyes. "I counted ten, Captain."

'Then − that was the last one!" Teggs said with relief. "The *Sauropod* was only carrying ten dung torpedoes."

"I'll shut down the Dung Magnet anyway," said Arx, pulling on the big golden lever. "The storerooms must be overflowing with droppings by now. If we draw in any more we will probably explode *without* the help of dung torpedoes!"

"But what about the star pirates?" said Teggs, banging his tail crossly against the floor. "Their space base might be super dirty now, but they will have gotten *clean* away!"

"Actually . . . no!" came a loud, high-pitched voice behind him.

The crewmembers sat up and cheered, and Teggs whirled round in surprise. "Hey, it's the Splarg!" he cried. "What are you doing here?"

The weird blobby, feathery monster with its three heads, two eyes and assorted noses did not look happy. "I wish to complain about the noise – and the fact that my pit is now knee-deep in dung. My special sing-a-sea-shanty night has been completely ruined, so I came up here to give you a piece of my mind." She paused. "And then I thought I might as well give you something else as well."

The Splarg opened one of her two enormous mouths, and the astrosaurs gasped.

Spiny Jim, Mutty, Pollysaurus – in fact, *all* the star pirates – were squashed up inside!

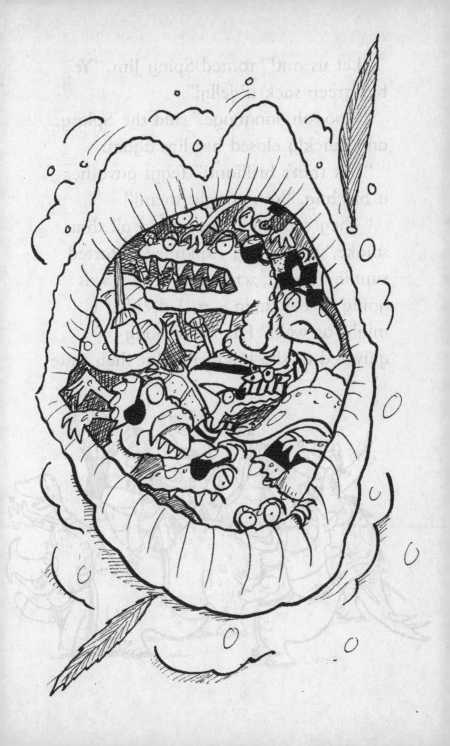

"Let us out!" roared Spiny Jim. "Ye big green sack o' jelly!"

"Oooooh, language," said the Splarg, and quickly closed her lips again.

"But that's brilliant!" Teggs gave her a big hug. "You caught them!"

"They ran right into me in all that smoke," the Splarg explained. "Started running about, screaming that I was going to eat them — so I decided I might as well!" Her huge body quivered as she laughed. "But they taste

so smelly and dirty and unwashed that I couldn't *possibly* swallow them."

The crewmembers started to applaud, and the astrosaurs joined in. Sprite flew over and preened one of her big red feathers with his beak. The Splarg gave a little curtsey, delighted by all the attention.

"Can you hold on to the star pirates until our ship gets here?" Teggs asked. "Then we can take them back to DSS HQ to face justice."

"I suppose so," said the Splarg.

Gipsy smiled. "I've just transmitted our exact position. The *Sauropod* will be here soon."

Sid punched the air. "That means we will be going home!"

"Yayyy!" cheered the other crewmembers.

"What about me?" said the Splarg sadly. "My pit is in pieces and I don't even know where my real home *is*."

Teggs looked around the gleaming room. "Well, to cheer you up, why don't you keep all the gold on board this space station? By catching the star pirates you have certainly earned it."

The Splarg gasped with her free mouth. "Really?"

Gipsy grinned. "You can build yourself a *lovely* home with all that loot!"

"I'll set up a fabulous café and nightclub," said the Splarg dreamily. "Singing nights every night! Free drinks for all my customers! I will never be lonely again!"

Iggy jabbed a thumb spike towards the star pirates in her spare mouth. "Shame Spiny Jim and his mates won't be able to drop in," he joked. "But I reckon they will be going to prison for a long time."

"Once they've cleaned up all the dungy mess their machine has left behind on Corytho," said Arx happily.

"A-harrr, Teggs," called Spiny Jim from inside the Splarg. "I has a request. Can I be having a solid gold prison cell, please? Stick the others where ye like, but give me a gold cell, me hearty!"

"You no-good rascal, Spiny Jim," said Mutty. "Just for that, I'm going to tell everyone your real name. It's not Jim at all. It's Gloria!"

"Not true!" the captain cried, but the other pirates were already laughing at him. "Curse the lot of ye!"

"Shut up, Spiny Gloria," sneered the raptor, and everyone laughed even harder — even the astrosaurs and their friends.

"Well now," said the Splarg, wiping her various eyes. "Since it's sing-a-sea-shanty night, how about a quick tune? I know just the ditty." And so, clearing her throats, she started to sing:

"I'll sing you a song
Of astrosaurs strong
And star pirates evil and naughty
The astrosaurs beat them
The Splarg she did eat them
So let's celebrate that they're caught—y!"

"I'll drink to that!" cried Iggy, leading the applause.

"Moss-juice all round!" said Sid, and everyone cheered.

"Make mine a large one," said Teggs, smiling at Arx, Iggy, Gipsy and Sprite. "This has certainly been an adventure to *treasure*. And I can't wait till we strike gold with another one, *me hearties* – HA-HARRR!"

THE END

ASTRO PUZZLE TIME

THE STAR PIRATES
QUIZ Questions

1. What was hidden in the cloud of black smoke?

2. Who was the leader of the pirates – and what was his real name?

3. What machines did the star pirates want in exchange for Arx and Teggs?

4. What did Pollysaurus the pterosaur fire at Captain Teggs?

5. What incredible device were the star pirates building?

Answers:

5. The Gold Magnet.

4. Dung pellets!

3. Two R-wave magnetrons.

2. Spiny Jim (secretly called Gloria).

1. The Star Pirates' massive space station.

ASTRO PUZZLE TIME

A-HARRRRD WORDSEARCH

```
D  T  E  G  G  S  S  J
S  A  E  X  J  P  X  P
W  G  L  R  L  I  A  A
O  E  M  A  G  N  E  T
R  M  R  O  N  Y  R  C
D  G  L  A  G  J  A  H
Y  D  S  R  P  I  T  R
O  Y  T  T  U  M  S  P
```

TEGGS
ARX
SWORD
SPINY JIM
ALAN
GOLD
MAGNET
MUTTY
SPLARG
PATCH
STAR
GEM

Can you find these twelve astro-tastic words in the word-maze above? Words may be hidden across, up, down and diagonally, forwards and backwards!

Meet the time-travelling cows!

THE TER-MOO-NATOR

BY STEVE COLE

IT'S 'UDDER' MADNESS!

Genius cow Professor McMoo and his trusty
sidekicks, Pat and Bo, are the star agents of the
C.I.A. –short for **COWS IN ACTION!** They travel through
time, fighting evil bulls from the future and
keeping history on the right track . . .

When Professor McMoo invents a brilliant **TIME
MACHINE**, he and his friends are soon attacked by a
terrifying **TER-MOO-NATOR** – a deadly robo-cow who
wants to mess with the past and change the future!
And that's only the start of an incredible **ADVENTURE**
that takes McMoo, Pat and Bo from a cow paradise
in the future to the **SCARY** dungeons
of King HenryVIII . . .

It's time for action. **COWS IN ACTION.**

JOIN THE SLIME SQUAD ON MORE
OF THEIR MISSIONS . . .

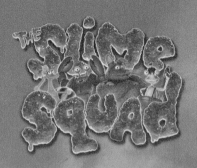

#1 ☐   #2 ☐   #3 ☐   #4 ☐

#5 ☐   #6 ☐   #7 ☐   #8 ☐